HEIDI

By
Johanna Spyri

Retold by
Colleen Reece

YOUNG READER'S CHRISTIAN LIBRARY

Illustrations by
Ken Save

A BARBOUR BOOK

HEIDI

"ARE YOU TIRED, HEIDI?"

1
Up the Mountain to Alm-Uncle

On a clear, sunny June morning a tall, strong girl led a child from the pleasant village of Mayenfeld up a winding footpath through shady green meadows into the stern, lofty mountains. The little girl's cheeks glowed crimson through her dark, sunburnt skin. No wonder. In spite of the hot sun, she wore three woolen dresses, a thick red shawl, and thick, nailed mountain-shoes, which were far too heavy for her five-year-old feet.

Halfway up the mountain, they came to the hamlet, Dorfli. Friends called greetings, but the tall girl kept walking until one cried, "Wait a minute, Dete. I'll go with you."

Dete stopped, and the child let go of her hand and sat on the ground. "Are you tired, Heidi?"

"No. I'm hot," she said, as she wearily rose up.

"We'll get to the top in another hour, if you take long steps," Dete said.

A stout, good-natured woman joined them, and Heidi fell back. The two friends talked. "This is the child your sister left?" the woman asked.

"Yes, Barbel. I am taking her to live with Alm-Uncle. I have the chance for a good place in Frankfurt. I'm not going to give it up."

"The child stay up there with Alm-Uncle! You must be out of your senses. The old man will send you and your proposal packing."

Dete tossed her head. "I've had charge of her until now. It's for him to do his duty. He's her grandfather. He won't harm her."

"She can't stay there!" Barbel said in horrified pity. "He has had nothing to do with anybody these long years and never sets foot inside a church. Why, his bushy eyebrows and immense beard are alarming enough. I should very much like to know what he has

"THIS IS THE CHILD YOUR SISTER LEFT?"

on his conscience to live like a hermit."

Dete hesitated and looked back to be sure the child couldn't overhear.

"She's climbing the slope yonder with the goat-herd and his goats. He can see after the child, and you can better tell me your tale."

"She doesn't need much looking after. She's smart for five. It will stand her in good stead some day, for the old man has nothing beyond his two goats and his hut. He once owned one of the largest farms of Domleschg, but lost it through drinking and gambling. His parents died of sorrow, and the younger brother, reduced to beggary, went off in anger. The Alm-Uncle disappeared for twelve or fifteen years. He reappeared with a young child, whom he tried to place with kinspeople but every door slammed in his face.

"Uncle came to Dorfli and lived with the boy, Tobias, who was a steady lad kindly received. The

"SHE'S SMART FOR FIVE"

wife and mother had died soon after her marriage. Tobias later married my sister, Adelaide, but died in an accident two years later. She fell into a fever and died soon after. Folks felt it to be a punishment from God which Uncle deserved for the godless life he had led. Some told him so. The minister begged him to repent. He refused; and then, we heard he had gone to live up the Alm and would never leave the mountain again. Mother and I took the little one, but now that Mother's gone, I have this excellent place."

"So, you are going to give the child over to the old man?" Reproach filled Barbel's voice, and she turned aside. "I leave you here."

Dete watched her go to a small, dark brown hut that stood in a hollow that afforded some protection from the mountain wind. Here lived Peter, the eleven-year-old boy who fetched the goats from Dorfli every morning. He drove them up to the mountains where they browsed till evening when he leaped

REPROACH FILLED BARBEL'S VOICE

down like one of his charges. A shrill whistle brought the owners to fetch their animals home. Peter lived alone with his mother, Brigitta, and a blind grandmother. His goat-herd father had been killed while cutting wood years before. Now, Dete started after the children, muttering at the delay.

Meanwhile, Heidi had panted and followed Peter until she couldn't bear her heavy, hot clothing. She pulled it off until she stood clad only in her light short-sleeved undergarment. Putting her clothes in a tidy heap, she scampered after the goat boy. Peter grinned when he saw her, but all too soon, Dete came up to them and shrieked,

"Heidi, what have you been doing! You good-for-nothing little thing!"

"I don't want any clothes." She stretched her arms in glee.

"Peter, go fetch her clothes," Dete ordered.

He didn't move. "I am already past my time." Not

"I DON'T WANT ANY CLOTHES"

until Dete held out a bright piece of new money did he skip down the steep mountain and return with the clothes. He carried them on up Alm mountain with Heidi and the goats skipping behind him.

When they reached the hut perched on its rock projection, Heidi went straight to the man with a long beard and thick gray eyebrows. "Good morning, Grandfather."

He abruptly shook her hand. "What's the meaning of this?"

"I have brought you Tobias and Adelaide's child," Dete said. "She is to remain here with you."

"And when the child begins to fret and whine after you, what am I to do?"

"That's your affair," retorted Dete.

"Then be off with you." He rose and glared.

"Good-bye," she hastily called and hurried down the mountain, to be met with accusing voices upbraiding her for leaving a helpless child with Alm-Uncle.

"WHAT'S THE MEANING OF THIS?"

HEIDI

Heidi looked about her with interest, then came to her grandfather who sat on a bench watching her. "I want to see inside the house."

"Come, then. Bring your bundle of clothes."

"I shan't want them any more. I want to go about like the goats."

The old man looked into her dark, sparkling eyes and saw intelligence there. "Do so if you like. We'll put your things in the cupboard."

Heidi followed him into a good-sized room, whose only furniture was a table, one chair, and the grandfather's bed in a corner. A hearth with a large kettle hanging above it stood in another corner. A large door in the wall opened to show a cupboard stocked with clothing and food. Heidi pushed her clothes far in and asked, "Where am I to sleep, Grandfather?"

"Wherever you like."

Delighted, she examined every nook and corner,

"WHERE AM I TO SLEEP, GRANDFATHER?"

then climbed a short ladder against the wall that led into the hay-loft. "I shall sleep here. It's lovely! I shall need a sheet." He brought a long, coarse quilt stuffed with hay and found a large, thick sack made of flax for a coverlid.

"I think we might have something to eat now," he told her. A few minutes later he had water boiling in the kettle over a clear, bright flame. He held a large piece of cheese on a long, iron fork till it toasted golden yellow. Heidi watched curiously, then turned and ran back and forth to the cupboard. She tidily laid out two plates and two knives. The grandfather put the steaming cheese on a layer of bread, then poured two bowls of milk. Heidi dragged a stool to the table, but it was too low. The old man placed her dinner on the one chair and put it before the three-legged stool.

"I never drank any milk so good before," Heidi said.

"I THINK WE MIGHT HAVE SOMETHING TO EAT NOW"

"Then you must have more." The grandfather poured more, and Heidi spread the butter-soft cheese on her bread and ate hungrily. After dinner, he put the goat-shed in order then took long round sticks, a small, round board and made a stool tall enough for Heidi to reach the table.

That evening, the wind began to roar through the old fir trees. Heidi clapped her hands and skipped around them. A shrill whistle came, then Peter arrived with the goats. Two goats, one brown and one white, ran to the grandfather, who stood holding a little salt for them. "Are they ours, Grandfather? Are you going to put them in the shed? Will they always stay with us?"

"Yes, yes. The white one is Little Swan. The brown one is Little Bear."

"Good night, Little Swan; good night, Little Bear," Heidi called. She sat down on the seat to eat and drink but the strong wind nearly blew her away.

HE MADE A STOOL TALL ENOUGH FOR HEIDI TO REACH THE TABLE

Soon, she climbed to her bed and slept as sweetly and soundly as any princess on a couch of silk.

While it was still twilight, the grandfather also went to bed, for he rose every morning at sunrise, which came very early during the summer months. The wind howled and wailed down the chimney like voices in pain. In the middle of the night, the grandfather got up. "The child will be frightened," he murmured. He mounted the ladder and stood by her bed.

Outside, the moon struggled with fast-driving clouds that first hid, then uncovered it. Just now, moonlight fell on Heidi's bed. She lay under the heavy coverlid, cheeks rosy with sleep, head peacefully resting on her round arm. Her face wore a happy expression, as if dreaming something pleasant. The old man looked down on the sleeping child until the moon again disappeared behind the clouds, and he could see no more. Then he went back to bed.

THE OLD MAN LOOKED DOWN ON THE SLEEPING CHILD

HE POINTED TO A LARGE TUB OF WATER BY THE DOOR

2
Out With the Goats

A loud whistle awakened Heidi. Golden sun rays poured through her round window that looked down into the valley. She jumped from bed, put on the few clothes she had taken off the night before, then climbed down the ladder and ran outside. Peter stood by the hut with his flock of goats, and the grandfather herded Little Swan and Little Bear out of the shed.

"If you want to go with Peter and the goats to the mountain, you must wash and make yourself tidy," the old man told her. "The sun that shines so brightly will laugh at you for being dirty." He pointed to a large tub of water by the door. She splashed and rubbed until she glistened, while the grandfather called Peter inside.

"Open your bag," he told the boy.

Peter obeyed. To his meager dinner, the grandfather added large pieces of bread and cheese, each twice the size of Peter's portions. He also put in a bowl. "You must milk two bowls for her," he ordered. "She cannot drink from the goats as you do. Take care she does not fall over the rocks, hear?"

Heidi ran in. "Will the sun laugh at me now?" she anxiously asked, red as a lobster from scrubbing.

He laughed. "No, but this evening, you will have to get in the tub like a fish. When you run about like the goats, you will get your feet dirty."

They started joyfully up the mountain. The wind had blown away the clouds. Dark, blue sky spread overhead, and the bright sun shone on the green slopes. Flowers opened their cups and looked up smiling. Heidi picked great handfuls and put them in her little apron.

Peter had to be alert, for the goats frisked as lively as did Heidi. "Where have you got to?" he called crossly.

"WHERE HAVE YOU GOT TO?"

"Here."

"Come, we have a long way to go. On the topmost peak, the old bird of prey sits and croaks. Besides, if you pick all the flowers now, there will be none for tomorrow."

They climbed until they reached the halting-place, where the plants the goats loved grew. On one side of the mountain, the rock split into deep clefts, and the grandfather had good reason to warn of danger. Peter threw himself on the warm ground, tired from his exertions.

Heidi sat down next to him. The valley lay far below. A great snow-field rose in front of them, with huge, bare rock peaks on either side. Peter fell asleep. Heidi had never been happier in her life. She heard a harsh cry. The largest bird she had ever seen with great spreading wings wheeled in wide circles.

"Peter, wake up. See, the bird!" Together, they watched it rise until it disappeared behind the gray mountain-tops.

"PETER, WAKE UP"

"It's gone home to its nest," Peter said. "Even the goats cannot climb that high." He whistled and called. Soon the goats sprang down the rocks and assembled on the green plateau. Some continued to nibble; others skipped about or pushed each other with their horns. Heidi played with them until Peter laid out their dinner and milked one of the goats.

"The milk is yours and the large pieces of bread and cheese," Peter said.

She drank two bowls of milk then broke her bread into two pieces, giving him the larger, and the whole big slice of cheese. "I have plenty." Peter looked astonished. Heidi laid the bread and cheese on his knees, and he saw she really meant for him to have them.

Between bites, he told her about the goats. Turk, with his big horns, was always butting the others. Most ran away, but Greenfinch, slender and nimble, bravely faced Turk and sometimes rushed him. Little

PETER LOOKED ASTONISHED

white Snowflake bleated so plaintively, Heidi ran and comforted her. Peter said Snowflake cried because the mother goat had been sold at Mayenfeld and would no longer come to the mountains.

Heidi clasped the animal. "Don't cry, you poor, little Snowflake. I'll come every day, and you won't have to be alone." She watched the goats climb the rocks again and decided Little Swan and Little Bear were the prettiest.

Suddenly, Peter leaped up and dashed through the flock. Greenfinch, the inquisitive, had sprung to the side of the mountain where the rocks went straight down to a great abyss. Peter threw himself down and grabbed one of her hind legs. Greenfinch bleated angrily and furiously. She struggled to free herself and tried to leap forward. "Heidi, help!" Peter cried.

She saw the danger they both were in, quickly gathered a bunch of sweet-smelling leaves and held

"HEIDI, HELP!"

them under Greenfinch's nose. The young animal turned and began eating the leaves. Peter got to his feet and between them, they led Greenfinch to safety. Peter raised his stick.

"No, you mustn't!" Heidi cried. She flung herself against him.

Peter looked at the flashing dark eyes and dropped his stick. "I'll let her off if you'll give me some more of your cheese tomorrow."

"You shall have it all tomorrow and every day, but you must promise never to beat Greenfinch or Snowflake or any of the goats." He agreed.

The day crept to its close. Heidi sprang up. "Why, Peter! Everything is on fire. The rocks and mountains and oh, look at the beautiful, fiery snow!"

"It's always like that. It will come again tomorrow," he told her when the rosy glow faded. Heidi silently followed him to her grandfather's hut. She promised Peter to go the next day. Then, she opened

"NO, YOU MUSTN'T!"

her apron and sadly exclaimed, "Grandfather, why do my flowers look so?"

"They like to stand out in the sun, not be shut up in an apron."

"Then I won't gather any more. Why does the great bird croak and scream?"

"The bird mocks the people who live huddled and gossiping in the villages. He calls, 'If you would go your own way come live on the heights, as I do.'"

Heidi told him of the world on fire.

The grandfather said, "When the sun says good night to the mountains, he throws his most beautiful colors over them, so they won't forget him before he comes again."

Day after day until autumn, Heidi went with Peter and the goats. Then the wind blew so hard, she could not go. The grandfather said a sudden gust of wind could blow her over the rocks into the valley below. Peter missed Heidi and found it dull on those days.

"THEY LIKE TO STAND OUT IN THE SUN"

The goats acted naughty, and he missed the good meals he'd had when she'd come.

Next came icy cold and such a heavy snowfall, not a single green leaf showed anywhere. Peter no longer came with the goats. More snow fell, until the window could not be opened. Heidi thought it great fun to be shut up in the hut with her grandfather. He shoveled the snow and piled it in mountain-like heaps around the house.

One afternoon, Peter came. He had fought his way through drifts and great lumps of snow had frozen to his clothes. He looked like a trickling waterfall when he stood by the fireplace to thaw.

"Well, General, now that you have lost your army, you must turn to pen and pencil. He goes to school winters, to learn how to read and write," the grandfather said. He fetched supper from the cupboard. Peter opened his round eyes wide when he saw the large piece of meat on his thick slice of

MORE SNOW FELL

bread. He seldom had such a nice thing to eat. "I shall come again next Sunday," he promised. "Grandmother sent word she would like you to come see her."

"The snow is too deep," answered the grandfather, but every day, Heidi said they must go, for the grandmother would be waiting. On the fourth day, the old man brought down Heidi's thick coverlid, climbed into a large hand-sleigh and took Heidi to his lap. Down, down the mountainside they shot, until they came to Peter's hut. "Go in, but when it begins to grow dark, start home." He went up the mountain, pulling the sleigh after him.

Heidi stepped into the tiny, dark cottage. Everything was poor and shabby, but clean. "Good day, Grandmother," Heidi said. "Grandfather brought me in the sleigh."

The old lady and Peter's mother could scarcely believe it. "What is she like, Brigitta?" the grand-

"GOOD DAY, GRANDMOTHER"

mother asked.

"Slender and dark with curly hair."

Heidi examined the room. "One of your shutters flaps. Grandfather could put in a nail, so it wouldn't bang and break one of the panes."

"I am not able to see it, but I can hear," the grandmother said. "Everything about this place rattles and creaks. Alas, Peter does not know how to fix it."

"If you were to go outside among all the snow, could you see the light?"

"It is always dark for me, but don't grieve, child. Talk to me."

So Heidi talked to the blind grandmother. She promised that her grandfather would come fix the shutter and make things right. Peter came in, and it was time for Heidi to go. She ran out. After a few steps, the grandfather appeared, carrying the warm sack.

When Peter told the grandmother, she said, "God

"IT'S ALWAYS DARK FOR ME, BUT DON'T GRIEVE, CHILD"

be thanked that he is good to her!" The next day, she again praised God when the Alm-Uncle came with hammer and nails.

Winter passed. Heidi brought brightness to the blind grandmother, who thanked God again and again for the child. In a home made cozy and secure by the grandfather's pounding, the old woman slept, untroubled by groanings and rattlings.

"GOD BE THANKED!"

HEIDI REMAINED LIGHTHEARTED AND HAPPY AS THE BIRDS

3
Heidi Leaves Her Friends

The seasons quickly passed. Heidi remained light-hearted and happy as the birds. She looked forward with delight to spring and the warm south wind that would roar and blow away the snow. At eight, Heidi knew all kinds of useful things. She could look after the goats as well as anyone. Little Swan and Little Bear followed her like two faithful dogs.

Twice during the winter, the schoolmaster sent word to the Alm-Uncle. Heidi must come to school. Uncle sent word back that he did not intend to send her.

The March sun melted the snow on the mountain side. Snowdrops bloomed. One sunny morning, Heidi had just jumped over the water-trough for the tenth time in her gladness, then fell back. An old gentleman dressed in black stood in front of her. "Don't be frightened," he said. "I am very fond of children. You must be Heidi. Where is your grandfather?"

"Sitting by the table, making round wooden spoons." Heidi opened the door.

The old village pastor from Dorfli had been a neighbor of Uncle's when he had lived in the village. "Good morning. It has been a long time since I saw you."

"Or I you." Surprised, the grandfather gave the visitor his chair. "Heidi, take the goats a little salt and stay till I come." She vanished.

"You know what has brought me here," the pastor said. "The child ought to have been at school a year ago. How are you going to let her grow up?"

"I am going to let her grow and be happy among the goats and birds. With them, she is safe and will learn nothing evil."

"The child is not a goat or bird. She cannot run wild and be ignorant. Next winter, she must come to

"THE CHILD OUGHT TO HAVE BEEN AT SCHOOL A YEAR AGO"

school every day."

"She will do no such thing." The old man ignored the visitor's rising anger. "Does the worthy pastor really mean he wishes me to send a young child miles down the mountains on ice-cold mornings through storm and snow? And let her return at night in raging winds when ones like ourselves run the risk of being blown down and buried in the snow? Have you forgotten her mother Adelaide, who was a sleep-walker and had fits? Might not the child do the same if obliged to over-exert herself? I will go before all the courts of justice in the country, and then we shall see who will force me to do it!"

"You are quite right, neighbor." The pastor sounded more friendly. "It is impossible for the child to come from here. I perceive she is dear to you. For her sake, do what you ought to have done long ago. Come down into Dorfli and live again among your fellowmen. What sort of life is this you lead, alone

"COME DOWN INTO DORFLI AND LIVE..."

and with bitter thoughts towards God and man!"

"The people in Dorfli despise me and I them."

"It is not good for you to be here. Seek to make peace with God, pray for forgiveness, and come see how differently people will look on you," the pastor said earnestly. He rose and held out his hand. "I wager that next winter you will be down among us again, and we shall be good neighbors, as of old."

Alm-Uncle gripped his hand but said firmly, "You mean well, but I will not send the child to school nor come live among you."

"Then God help you!" The pastor sadly left and went down the mountain.

The next day, Cousin Dete arrived. She wore a fine, feathered hat and a long, trailing skirt that swept the floor of the hut. She plunged into the reason for her visit. "Heidi is looking well, but some immensely wealthy relatives of those I serve in Frankfurt need a child. Their young daughter is an

"THEN GOD HELP YOU!"

invalid and goes about in a wheelchair. Heidi is to be her companion. Why, great things are in store for her, if they take a fancy to Heidi. If anything happens to the weak child—"

"I will have nothing to do with it."

Dete leaped from her seat like a rocket. "The child is now eight years old, and you will not let her learn, or send her to church or school. She is my own sister's child. There are certain things I can bring up in court about you. Not one person will take your part against me!"

"Be silent!" thundered Uncle. "Never let me see you again with your hat and feather and such words on your tongue!" He strode out.

"You have made Grandfather angry," Heidi said.

"He will soon be all right. Show me where your clothes are."

"I'm not coming." Her dark eyes looked unfriendly.

"BE SILENT!"

"Nonsense! Your grandfather wants you to go with me. If you do not like it, you can come back again. He will be in good temper by that time."

On the way down the mountain, they saw Peter, who had stolen a holiday from school. Heidi told him she was going to Frankfurt. Peter banged into the hut and told his grandmother. She grew agitated and cried, "Dete, Dete, do not take the child away from us!"

Heidi struggled to get free. "Grandmother is calling. I must go to her!" Dete had no intention of allowing the child to stay. She promised Heidi could bring back soft rolls of white bread for the grandmother who could hardly eat the hard, black bread. The child was so glad she ran ahead, believing they could get back from Frankfurt before night.

From that day forward, Alm-Uncle looked fiercer and more forbidding than ever when he passed through Dorfli carrying his pack of cheeses on his

"I MUST GO TO HER!"

back. The gossip grew more and more wild. Only the blind grandmother praised him for his kindness in mending the house. Those in Dorfli said she must be mistaken. The old blind woman murmured, "Alas, all our happiness has gone with the child. The days are long and dreary. Pray God, I see Heidi once again before I die!"

Clara Sesemann lay on her invalid couch. Thin and pale, her blue eyes gazed at the clock. "Isn't it time yet, Fraulein Rottenmeier?"

The lady-housekeeper had been in sole charge all the years since Clara's mother had died. Her shoulder-cape and dome-shaped head dress gave her a certain solemnity. When Tinette, the maid, ushered Dete and Heidi in, Fraulein rose and haughtily stared at the child in the plain, woolen frock and bent, straw hat. "What is your name?"

"Heidi."

"HEIDI"

"That's no Christian name."

"The child is unaccustomed to strangers." Dete poked Heidi. "She does not know good manners but is docile and willing to learn. She was christened Adelaide, after her dead mother."

"That's a name one can pronounce, but Dete, I am astonished. Fraulein Clara is over twelve. What age is this child? I want a young lady to share lessons."

"I think she is about ten," Dete began.

"Grandfather told me I was eight," Heidi put in. Dete poked her again.

Fraulein Rottenmeier cried angrily, "Four years too young! What books did you learn from?"

"None. I have never learnt to read."

"How could you bring me a child like this?" Fraulein turned on Dete, who airily replied that she must go. She bowed and escaped. Fraulein ran after her.

"HOW COULD YOU BRING ME A CHILD LIKE THIS?"

"Come here," Clara said. "I will call you Heidi. Are you pleased to be here?"

"No. I shall go home tomorrow and take Grandmother a white loaf."

"What a funny child! You aren't going home, but will live with me and our tutor will teach you to read."

Heidi said nothing until Sebastian, the butler, flung open the dining room doors. "Why, you look like Peter," she cried.

Fraulein Rottenmeier clasped her hands in horror. "Now she is addressing the servant as if he were a friend! I never imagined such a child."

A soft white roll lay by Heidi's dinner place. She put it in her pocket. Sebastian wanted to laugh. Heidi fell asleep during Fraulein Rottenmeier's long list of rules and manners and earned the housekeeper's wrath.

In the following days, she innocently kept the

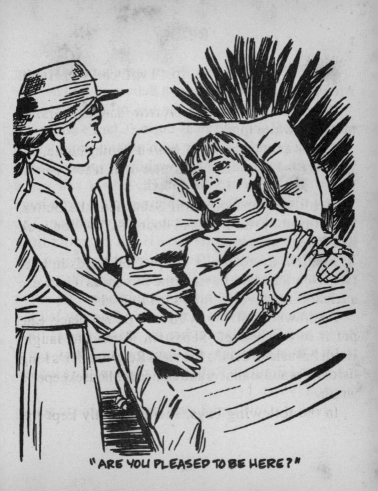

"ARE YOU PLEASED TO BE HERE?"

household in an uproar. When she couldn't see her mountains from the window, Sebastian told her she would have to climb to the top of a high church tower. Heidi skipped away during Clara's afternoon nap. She promised a boy with a hand-organ and a monkey that Clara would give him twopence if he'd show her the way to the church. All she saw was a sea of roofs, towers, and chimney pots, but a huge gray cat in a large basket caught her attention. The church keeper promptly gave Heidi the entire litter of squirming kittens. "I will bring them to you, but you may take two now," he said.

Heidi put a white kitten in one pocket, a yellow and white striped one in the other. The boy led her home and Sebastian let her in. "Make haste, little miss. Go straight into the dining room. They are at table, and Fraulein Rottenmeier looks like a loaded cannon."

Heidi slid into her place. Fraulein began to scold.

FRAULEIN BEGAN TO SCOLD

Meow.

"How dare you answer me so, Adelheid?"

"I didn't—"

Meow. Meow.

"Leave this room at once."

"It isn't I, it's the kittens—"

"Kittens!" Fraulein shrieked. "Sebastian, take the horrid things away!" She rushed into the study and locked the door.

Clara ordered Sebastian to make a bed for the kittens. He set to work, knowing there would be a further rumpus. But Fraulein held off on her sermon, too exhausted to give it!

"IT ISN'T I, IT'S THE KITTENS—"

"I SAW HER IN THE STREET"

4
A Great Commotion in the Large House

Sebastian ran to answer a loud ring at the bell the next morning. Only Herr Sesemann rang like that. He must have returned unexpectedly.
Instead, a ragged little boy carrying a hand-organ said, "I want to see Clara."

"You dirty, good-for-nothing rascal! What do you want of her?"

"She owes me fourpence."

"You must be out of your mind!" Sebastian roughly said.

"She owes me twopence for showing her the way there and twopence for showing her the way back."

"What a pack of lies! Miss Clara never goes out. She cannot walk."

"I saw her in the street. She has short, curly black hair and black eyes."

Oho, thought Sebastian. *Little Miss has been up to more mischief.* He led the way to the study, telling the urchin to play his organ the instant he got inside the room, for the young lady loved music.

From the dining room, Fraulein Rottenmeier heard the street music and rushed to the study where the ragged boy turned away at his organ and the children shook with laughter. She shouted for him to leave off and dashed toward him. Then she saw a dreadful, dark tortoise crawling toward her feet! She leaped higher than she had for years and screamed, "Sebastian!"

The organ-player stopped. Sebastian stood outside bent double with laughter, peering in at the scene. He stepped inside. Fraulein commanded, "Get them away!" and sank to a chair. Sebastian ushered the boy out and gave him fourpence for showing Heidi the way and fourpence for his music!

Quietness fell over the study, but soon another

"SEBASTIAN!"

knock sounded at the door. Sebastian came in with a large covered basket. "Finish the lessons before unpacking the basket," Fraulein Rottenmeier ordered, but Clara teased,

"May I just have one peep inside?" Her tutor agreed, and she opened the basket.

One, two, three—two more—then even more kittens tumbled out and raced through the room. They jumped over the tutor's boots, climbed Fraulein's dress and sent her into hysterics. Clara exclaimed, "The dear things! Heidi, just see," while the younger girl chased this one and that.

At last, Fraulein found her voice. She screeched for Sebastian and Tinette. The kittens were gathered up, and the housekeeper furiously turned to Heidi. "This is all your fault, you utter barbarian! Into the dark cellar with rats and black beetles, you'll go until you're tamed."

Heidi had never seen such a place. The grandfather's cellar held fresh made cheeses and new

"INTO THE DARK CELLAR WITH RATS AND BLACK BEETLES, YOU'LL GO"

milk. Neither did she know about rats and black beetles.

Distressed, Clara interrupted. "No, Fraulein. You must wait for Papa."

"I will have something to say to Herr Sesemann," she threatened.

Two peaceful days followed, but Fraulein Rottenmeier felt never again would there be peace. She plotted how to get rid of Heidi.

In the meantime, the child always pocketed her white rolls at dinner and supper, saving them so the grandmother wouldn't have to eat hard, black bread. She had learned she must not talk with the kindly Sebastian at the table. Scornful Tinette turned up her nose. Heidi could not run about as she did at home.

One day, she felt she could bear it no longer. Dete had said she could go home whenever she chose. So she tied all the rolls in her red shawl, put on her straw

ONE DAY, SHE FELT SHE COULD BEAR IT NO LONGER

hat and went downstairs.Unfortunately, she met Fraulein Rottenmeier at the hall door.

"Where do you think you're going? Haven't I told you not to run about?"

"I'm not running about. I am going home," Heidi said.

"Home!" Fraulein threw her hands in the air. "You have everything you could possibly want here, you naughty, ungrateful thing!"

"I only want to go home." Heidi poured forth her troubles. "If I stay away so long, Snowflake will cry, and the grandmother is waiting. I can never see here how the sun says good-night to the mountains. If the great bird flew over Frankfurt, he would croak louder than ever."

"Heaven have mercy on us, she is out of her mind." Fraulein hurried inside. "Sebastian, bring that unhappy little creature in at once."

Heidi stood with eyes aflame, trembling all over.

" I AM GOING HOME "

HEIDI

"What, in trouble again?" Sebastian asked. He put a kindly hand on her shoulder. "There, there, don't take it to heart so much, and don't let her bully you. The kittens love their new home. Later, we'll go see them." But Heidi slowly went upstairs, so joyless it touched Sebastian's heart.

The next day, Fraulein Rottenmeier told the tutor of Heidi's strange speech. He replied the child was eccentric, and he feared she could not learn, but she wasn't mad.

Meanwhile, Fraulein thought of Heidi's shabby garments and went to sort them, intending to make over some of Clara's dresses and hats. She returned with an expression of horror. "Adelaide, what is this I find in your wardrobe but a great pile of rolls! Tinette, go upstairs, take away all that bread, and throw out the old straw hat."

"No!" screamed Heidi. "I need the hat, and the rolls are for the grandmother!" She ran to stop

"THERE, THERE, DON'T TAKE IT TO HEART SO MUCH"

Tinette but Fraulein grabbed her. Heidi pulled free and threw herself on Clara's couch. "Now Grandmother won't have them. They were for her." She cried as if her heart would break.

"Don't cry," Clara comforted. "I promise you shall have even more rolls, all nice and fresh, when you go home. Yours would be hard and stale by then." Still it took a long time for Heidi to stop weeping.

At supper, she sobbed when she saw the roll, but Sebastian mysteriously whispered, "Don't be unhappy. I have it safe for you." That night she found her old straw hat where he had hidden it under her counterpane and stuffed it far back in her cupboard.

A few days later, Herr Sesemann returned. After affectionately greeting Clara, he turned. "And this is our little Swiss girl. Tell me, are you and Clara good friends?"

"Oh, yes," they chorused.

"ARE YOU AND CLARA GOOD FRIENDS?"

"I must have my dinner, then I will show you what I brought," he promised. He found Fraulein Rottenmeier in the dining room.

"Herr Sesemann," she said. "You remember that we decided to get a well-behaved companion for Clara. I have been shockingly, disgracefully imposed on. If you only knew the kind of people and animals the child has brought into the house during your absence! She must not be in her right mind. The tutor agrees with me." She called him in, and he said Heidi should not be wholly condemned; she had been brought up in an unusual manner.

Herr Sesemann interrupted. "Is she a fit companion for my daughter?"

The tutor stammered and Herr Sesemann cut him short and went to his daughter. "Child," he told Heidi. "Will you fetch me a glass of water, fresh as you can get it?"

She skipped away and he asked his daughter,

"SHE MUST NOT BE IN HER RIGHT MIND"

"What has she done that Fraulein thinks her not in her right mind?" He laughed heartily at the story of the kittens and listened when Clara begged him not to send Heidi away. When she came back in he asked, "Is this fresh?"

"Fresh from the pump. I had to go a long way," Heidi said. "There were such a lot of people at the first pump and just as many at the second. I got water at the one in the next street. The gentleman with white hair asked me to give kind regards to you after I told him I was taking the water to Herr Sesemann."

"I wonder who sent me such good wishes," he pondered.

"He was kind and laughed. He had a thick gold chain with a gold thing hanging from it with a large red stone," Heidi reported. "His stick had a horse's head at the top."

"It's my old friend the doctor," Clara exclaimed. Herr Sesemann smiled to himself at what his friend's

"IS THIS FRESH?"

opinion must be of this new way of getting water!

That evening, he told Fraulein Rottenmeier he had found Heidi in a perfectly right state of mind, and his daughter wanted to keep her as a companion. "She is to be kindly treated. My mother will shortly come for a long visit, and she can get on with anybody."

Fraulein felt no relief at the thought of the coming help.

Before the fortnight ended, Herr Sesemann comforted Clara with the prospect of her grandmother's arrival and left again to attend to business in Paris. He had just gone when a letter came from Frau Sesemann saying she would be there the following day. A carriage should be sent to meet her at the station. Clara talked so much about her grandmother, Heidi began to call her "grandmamma." This brought a look of displeasure from Fraulein Rottenmeier. Heidi didn't pay much attention. She

"SHE IS TO BE KINDLY TREATED"

had grown accustomed to the housekeeper's black looks.

That night, Fraulein waylaid Heidi and drew her into her own room. She gave strict orders on how to address Frau Sesemann when she arrived. On no account was Heidi to call her "grandmamma" but must always say "madam" to her. "Do you understand?" she asked when she saw a perplexed expression on the child's face. Heidi had not understood, but seeing Fraulein's severe look, she didn't ask for more explanation.

HEIDI HAD NOT UNDERSTOOD

"IS THAT HOW THEY ADDRESS PEOPLE IN YOUR MOUNTAINS?"

5
Another Grandmother

The next morning, Fraulein Rottenmeier went about upright and dignified, showing her authority would continue in spite of Frau Sesemann's coming. She sent Heidi to her room and ordered her to remain there, so Clara could see her grandmother alone first. Soon, Tinette summoned her.

"Ah, here comes the child! Come along and let me have a good look at you," a kindly voice said.

"Good evening." Eager to follow instructions, Heidi added, "Mrs. Madam."

"Well, is that how they address people in your mountains?" She laughed.

"No, I never knew anyone with that name before," Heidi said gravely.

"Nor I either." Frau Sesemann patted her cheek and laughed again. "Never mind. When I am with children, I am always grandmamma." She looked more closely at Heidi and nodded. "What is your name?"

The child looked back into the grandmother's face and at her beautiful white hair and the lace on her cap. "I am always called Heidi, but I am now to be called Adelaide—" she broke off when Fraulein Rottenmeier entered.

"Frau Sesemann will no doubt agree with me that it was necessary to choose a name that could be pronounced easily, if only for the servants' sake."

"My worthy Rottenmeier," the old lady replied. "If a person is called Heidi and is accustomed to that name, I call her by the same, so let it be."

It always annoyed Fraulein that Frau Sesemann continually addressed her by her surname only, but the grandmother followed her own way.

The next day, while Clara slept, the grandmother went to Fraulein's room. "Where is the child, and

"IF A PERSON IS CALLED HEIDI... I CALL HER BY THE SAME"

what is she doing all this time?"

"Sitting in her room where she could well employ herself if she had the least idea of being useful. You have no idea of the out-of-the-way things this child imagines and does. I could hardly repeat them in good society."

"I should do the same if I had to sit in there like that child; I doubt if you would then like to repeat what *I* did in good society," she retorted. "Go fetch the child to my room. I have some pretty books for her."

"That is the misfortune." Fraulein made a despairing gesture. "She has not even been able to learn her ABC's. If the tutor had not the patience of an angel, he would have given up teaching her long ago."

"She does not look to me like a child unable to learn her alphabet." Frau Sesemann cut short Fraulein Rottenmeier's further remarks, and soon Heidi ap-

SHE GAZED WIDE-EYED AT THE PICTURES

peared. She gazed wide-eyed at the pictures ther
tears came and led to sobs. One picture showed a
green pasture filled with young animals, some graz
ing, others nibbling at shrubs. In the middle, a
shepherd leaned on his staff. Golden light from the
sinking sun bathed the whole scene.

"Don't cry." Grandmamma patted her hand. "The
picture has perhaps reminded you of something, bu
there is a beautiful tale I will tell you this evening
Come, dry your tears. We must have a little talk.'
When Heidi grew calmer, Grandmamma asked, "Ar
you getting on well in your lessons?"

"Oh, no." Heidi sighed. "I knew beforehand, i
was not possible to learn. Peter told me. He tried an
tried but could not learn to read."

"Peter must be a very odd boy, then. Listen
Heidi, you can learn to read in a very little while
You see that picture with the shepherd and animals
As soon as you can read, the book will be your own.

"IT WAS NOT POSSIBLE TO LEARN"

"If I could only read now!" she exclaimed and brightened a bit.

Yet, since the day Heidi had tried to go home, a change had come over her. She at last understood she would have to stay in Frankfurt for a long time, perhaps forever. Fraulein Rottenmeier had told her Herr Sesemann would think it ungrateful if she wished to leave. She believed Clara and Grandmamma would feel the same way, so she had no one to talk to. She could no longer eat and grew paler every day. She lay awake at night, then fell asleep to dream of rocks and the snow-field turned crimson in the evening light, of sunshine and flowers. She woke, thinking herself back in the hut, only to find the room in Frankfurt far away from home. She often laid her face on the pillow and wept long and quietly so no one would hear.

Grandmamma saw Heidi's unhappiness and asked her about it.

"I cannot tell you or Clara or anyone."

"I CANNOT TELL YOU OR CLARA OR ANYONE"

HEIDI

"Dear child, let me tell you what to do. When we are in great trouble and cannot speak to anybody, we must turn to God and pray Him to help, for He can deliver us. You say your prayers every evening to the dear God in heaven and thank Him for all He has done for you, and pray Him to keep you from all evil, do you not?"

Heidi shook her head. "No, I never say any prayers. I used to with my first grandmother, but that was a long time ago. I have forgotten them."

"That is why you are so unhappy. Think of the comfort when a heart heavy with grief goes and tells it to God. He can give us everything that will make us happy again."

A gleam of joy came to the child's eyes. "May I tell Him *everything*?" When the old lady nodded, she quickly asked, "May I go?" She ran to her room, sat on a stool and told God everything that made her so sad and unhappy. She begged Him earnestly to help

"THAT IS WHY YOU ARE SO UNHAPPY"

her and let her go home to her grandfather.

About a week later, the tutor came to Frau Sesemann. "It is truly marvelous. The child who never seemed able to learn her ABC's has started to read!"

Grandmamma went to the study. Heidi sat beside Clara, reading aloud. That evening, the large book with the beautiful pictures lay on her plate and Grandmamma said it was hers to keep always, even when she went home. Clara put in, "You aren't going home yet, Heidi, not for years."

Heidi loved the book, but best of all, was the picture of the shepherd, happy among his father's sheep and goats. Next, came a picture showing him far away from his father's house, thin and pale, eating with the pigs. The third picture was the old father running with outstretched arms to embrace his repentant son who advanced timidly, worn and wearing a ragged coat. Heidi never tired of

HEIDI LOVED THE BOOK

Grandmamma's explaining the story to her and Clara.

The time drew near for Frau Sesemann to return home. Although she liked to hear Heidi read aloud, she saw the child never looked really happy. A few days before her departure, Grandmamma called Heidi aside. "Have you the same trouble at heart? Have you told God about it? Do you pray every day?"

"No, I have left off praying. It is of no use. God does not listen. I prayed the same thing every day for weeks, and yet He has not done what I asked."

"Child, God is a good father. He knows better than we do, what is good for us. He gives something better than what we ask for if we do not run away and lose our trust in Him. When God no longer hears the voice of one He knew among those who pray to Him, He lets that person go her own way until she gets in trouble. Then she cries, 'Save me, God. There is none other to help me.' Will you not trust

"CHILD, GOD IS A GOOD FATHER"

Him and ask Him to forgive you? You may be sure He will make everything right and happy for you."

Heidi had perfect confidence in the grandmother, and she cried, "I will go at once and ask Him to forgive me. I will never forget Him again."

"That is right, dear child. Don't be unhappy. He will do everything you wish in good time."

The day Grandmamma left, the house stood silent and felt empty. When Heidi began to read to Clara, it didn't last long. The tale about a dying grandmother brought a burst of tears. "Oh, then Grandmother is dead. I shall never see her again, and she never had the white rolls!" Clara did all she could to explain that the story was about a different grandmother. Yet, after Heidi stopped weeping, she couldn't help being afraid the blind grandmother and even her grandfather might die. If she did not go home for a long time, she would find everything silent and dead. She would be all alone.

"I WILL NEVER FORGET HIM AGAIN"

HEIDI

Fraulein Rottenmeier swept in. "Adelaide, that is enough. If there are any more scenes like this, I shall take the book and not let you have it again."

Heidi clutched her treasure but often made faces to hold back her tears. She lost her appetite. Sebastian could hardly bear to have her refuse the nice dishes he handed her. All his pleading proved useless. At night, the picture of home rose before her eyes. She wept, again hiding her face in her pillow.

Many weeks passed. Heidi didn't know if it was winter or summer. The walls and windows she looked out on showed no change, and she and Clara seldom went beyond the house. Autumn and winter went by. Again the sun came shining on the white walls of the opposite houses. Heidi told herself, "It's time for Peter to go out again with the goats to the flowers and glowing sunset." She huddled in a corner of her lonely room and put her hands over her eyes to shut out the sun shining on the opposite wall.

SHE HUDDLED IN A CORNER OF HER LONELY ROOM

HEIDI

There she sat, not moving but silently battling with her terrible homesickness until Clara sent for her again.

THERE SHE SAT

WHAT WAS THAT SOUND?

6
A Ghost in the House!

Fraulein Rottenmeier crept about from room to room, peering into the dark corners. She would not go alone into the upper floor grand guest-chambers or down into the mysterious council-chamber. Neither would Tinette or Sebastian. Something strange and mysterious had begun in Herr Sesemann's house.

Every morning when the servants went downstairs, the front door stood open. A great alarm rose. Yet nothing had been touched! How could a door doubly locked at night with a wooden bar fastened across it be opened? Fraulein Rottenmeier persuaded Sebastian and John to stay up and watch.

Alas, they grew sleepy. When midnight struck, Sebastian awakened. *What was that sound*? He shook John who courageously said, "Come, we must go outside." He opened the door and stepped into the hall. A sudden gust of wind blew through the open front door and put out the light in John's hand. He fell back, nearly upset Sebastian, then clutched the butler and jerked him back into the room. John slammed the door, turned the key, and relighted his candle. Sebastian gave a cry of alarm. John trembled all over, white as a ghost. "I saw a white figure at the top of the steps—then it disappeared!"

Sebastian felt his blood run cold. Neither man dared move till morning. The instant they told Fraulein, she wrote to Herr Sesemann. Dreadful and unaccountable things were happening. He must come at once.

He wrote back he could not leave his business and expressed astonishment at the ghost tale. He said if further disturbances came, Fraulein should write to the grandmother and bid her come deal with the ghost.

A plea to Frau Sesemann brought a sharp

SEBASTION FELT HIS BLOOD RUN COLD

reproof. "I am not inclined to come to Frankfurt because you fancy you see ghosts, Rottenmeier," she wrote. "There has never been a ghost in the house. If there is now, it must be a live one. If you cannot deal with it, send for the watchman."

Fraulein went straight to the children and told them about the ghost.

Clara screamed she would not stay a minute alone. Fraulein and Heidi must sleep in her room and keep a light burning. Her father must come home!

Fraulein said they could not all sleep in the same room. She would come to Clara and Tinette to Heidi. Heidi was far more frightened of the haughty Tinette than any ghost and said she'd rather be alone. Fraulein immediately wrote to Herr Sesemann that the goings-on in the house had so affected his daughter, she could be expected to have fits.

Two days later, he arrived. Clara told him she had nothing the matter with her and was glad about the

TWO DAYS LATER, HE ARRIVED

ghost for it had brought him home. Herr Sesemann turned to Fraulein Rottenmeier. "How is the ghost?"

"You will not laugh tomorrow morning," she told him and swept out.

Herr Sesemann called Sebastian aside. "Lad, have you been playing tricks?"

"No, on my honor."

Punctually at nine o'clock, after the children and Fraulein had retired, Herr Sesemann's old friend the doctor arrived in answer to a summons. "You look pretty bad for a person I am to sit up with all night."

"Patience, friend. The one we sit up for will look worse when we catch him. I have a ghost in the house!"

Herr Sesemann recounted the story of the open front door. He brought forth two loaded revolvers. A shot in the air would frighten the intruder.

When the clock struck twelve, the doctor yawned but Herr Sesemann said, "Wait a bit. It doesn't

"HOW IS THE GHOST?"

generally appear before one."

Just after the clock's single chime sounded, the front door bar slid aside, and the key turned in the lock. The door opened. Armed with revolvers and lights, the two men stepped into the hall. Moonlight shone on a motionless white figure in the open doorway.

"Who is there?" thundered the doctor. The men advanced.

The figure turned and gave a low cry. There in her little white nightgown, Heidi stood trembling, staring at the lights and revolvers.

"Why, it's your little water-carrier."

"Child, what does this mean?" Herr Sesemann asked.

Terrified, hardly able to speak, Heidi answered, "I don't know."

The doctor stepped forward, "Don't be frightened." He laid down the revolver and gently took Heidi's

"WHY, IT'S YOUR LITTLE WATER CARRIER"

hand. Once he got her back into bed, he said, "Where were you wanting to go?"

"I did not want to go anywhere. I had been dreaming. I do every night. I think I am back with Grandfather. I see the stars shining and hear the wind in the fir trees. I open the door and run out, and it is all so beautiful. When I wake, though, I am still in Frankfurt."

"Have you no pain?"

"Only the feeling a great stone weighs on me here." She pressed her hand to her heart. "As if I wanted to cry, but Fraulein forbade it."

The doctor questioned her until Heidi broke into violent weeping. He told her to go ahead and cry— it would do her good—then go to sleep. "It will all be right tomorrow," he promised. Then he sought out his friend. "Your little charge is your ghost and a sleepwalker. She is consumed with homesickness and is nearly a skeleton. Tomorrow, you must send her home."

"YOUR LITTLE CHARGE IS YOUR GHOST AND A SLEEPWALKER"

"What!" Herr Sesemann rose and paced the room. "Homesick and ill in my house? How can I send the child who came here happy and healthy back to her grandfather in such condition? Make her whole, then she shall go home."

"This illness cannot be cured with pills and powders. If you send her at once, she may recover in the mountain air. Better to send her ill than not at all!"

Shocked, Herr Sesemann vowed, "It will be seen to at once." He roused the servants from their beds, went to his daughter and told her Heidi must go home in order to get well. Distressed, Clara pleaded but Herr Sesemann shook his head. "Make no further fuss, and I will take you to Switzerland next summer," he promised.

Clara gave in and asked that Heidi's box be brought to her room. Herr Sesemann sent for Sebastian and told him to take Heidi home. He had never seen such delight as that in Heidi's face once

"BETTER TO SEND HER ILL THAN NOT AT ALL!"

she realized she really, truly was going back to her mountains and beloved friends and pets. Her eyes rounded when Clara said, "See what I have put in? Dresses and aprons and handkerchiefs and just look." She held up a basket. Inside lay twelve beautiful round white rolls, all for the blind grandmother.

Heidi ran to her room and gathered up her book and old red shawl. Fraulein tried to take it from her, but Herr Sesemann scowled and Heidi kept the shawl.

Once in the railway carriage, she said, "Sebastian, are you sure Grandmother on the mountain is not dead?"

"She is alive," he told her. "There is no reason for her to be dead."

First, by railway, then by shabby cart and horse, Heidi traveled back to Dorfli. She carried her basket and a letter from Herr Sesemann. The trunk rode behind her in the cart. The driver asked curiously,

HEIDI TRAVELED BACK TO DORFLI

"Didn't they treat you well?"

"Oh, yes, but I would a thousand times rather be with Grandfather on the mountain than anywhere else in the world," she told him. They reached the village at five. Many tried to stop and question her, telling her how much worse the Alm-Uncle had been the past year. Heidi pushed through them and ran up the steep path as fast as the heavy basket allowed. She found the grandmother in her corner. "I have really come back, and I am never going away again." She put the soft rolls in the old woman's lap.

"What a blessing you bring, but you are the greatest blessing, child." Tears fell from the blind eyes.

Heidi would not stay long but promised to come the next day. She remembered Grandfather telling Dete he never wanted to see her hat or feathers again and gave her own pretty hat to Brigitta. She took off her city dress, put her red shawl on over her

"I AM NEVER GOING AWAY AGAIN"

petticoat, donned the old straw hat she had wrapped in the shawl and started home. The beautiful red glow she loved painted the mountains, rocks, and sky. "Oh, God, thank you for bringing me home," she called, then hurried to the little hut.

Grandfather sat on the porch as in the old days. She rushed to him, flung her arms about him and cried, "Grandfather, Grandfather" again and again.

The old man said nothing. He passed his hand over his wet eyes. "So you have come back to me. Did they send you away?"

"Oh, no. I think it's all in the letter." She ran to fetch it.

Soon after, Peter's shrill whistle announced his arrival with the goats. She ran to him and then to greet the goats. Even shy little Snowflake butted the Great Turk out of the way to reach her. She promised to go with Peter soon.

That night, Heidi lay down on her freshly made

"SO YOU HAVE COME BACK TO ME"

hay bed with a happy heart. She slept more soundly than she had done in a whole year. Her grandfather got up at least ten times to see if she was all right. Heidi did not stir. She had no need to wander about. The great, burning longing of her heart had been satisfied. She'd seen the high mountains and rocks alight in the evening glow. She had heard the wind in the fir trees. Best of all, she was at home again on the mountain.

SHE WAS AT HOME AGAIN ON THE MOUNTAIN

"GRANDMOTHER, I CAN READ NOW"

7
A Sunday Surprise for Heidi

Saturday afternoon, the Alm-Uncle accompanied Heidi to the grandmother's. "Is it you, child?" the old woman called. "I feel stronger already from having the wonderful white rolls."

"She has only eaten one so far," Brigitta said. "She is afraid she will come to the end of them. If only I could pay for those the baker in Dorfli makes."

"Grandmother, I have lots of money. The Sesemanns sent it in the letter. I will buy you a fresh white roll every day and two on Sunday. Peter can bring them up from Dorfli." She refused to listen to the grandmother's protests.

Suddenly, she caught sight of the grandmother's songbook. "Grandmother, I can read now." She climbed on a chair, lifted down the book, and wiped away the dust. Heidi chose a hymn about the sun and

God's handiwork. She finished with the words, "Joy shall be ours, in that garden blest, where after storm we find our rest. I wait in peace—God's time is best."

"Heidi, that brings light to my heart." The old woman's face was alight with peace and joy, as if she were already looking with new, clear eyes into the garden of Paradise.

All the way home, Heidi chattered. "Grandfather, will you give all the money to me? I can give Peter enough for the grandmother's rolls."

"It would be nice for you to have a proper bed, and there would still be plenty for the bread," he told her.

Heidi laughed. "I sleep better on my bed of hay."

"Then you may buy bread for the grandmother for years to come."

Heidi shouted with joy, sang, and skipped, then quieted. "If God had let me come at once when I

"IT WOULD BE NICE FOR YOU TO HAVE A PROPER BED"

prayed and wept, I should only have had a little bread. I should not have been able to read, which is a comfort to Grandmother. God arranged it all so much better than I knew how. Everything happened just as the other grandmother said it would. Now we will pray every day, won't we, and never forget Him again."

"Supposing one does forget Him," said the old man.

"Then everything goes wrong, for God lets us go where we like."

"No one can go back. He whom God has forgotten is forgotten forever."

"Oh, no, we can go back! Grandmamma told me, and I will read it to you from my beautiful book." She struggled faster up the steep slope, ran into the hut, and came out with the book. She began the story of the son happy at home who wanted to be his own master and have his own goods and money. She read

"HE WHOM GOD HAS FORGOTTEN IS FORGOTTEN FOREVER"

how he wasted all his father gave him and hired out to watch swine. He wore rags and had just a few husks to eat, until he repented and said, "'I will arise and go to my Father.'" She told of the wonderful way the father ran to meet the son who cried, "'Father, I have sinned against heaven and before thee and am not worthy to be called thy son.'" Then, she pointed to the prodigal standing by the father who had run to greet him. "Isn't it wonderful?"

"Yes, Heidi." That night, Grandfather climbed the ladder and put his lamp down so the light fell on the child. Heidi's hands lay folded as if she had fallen asleep saying her prayers. An expression of peace and trust rested on her face. At last, he also folded his hands. With bowed head, he said in a low voice, "Father, I have sinned against heaven and before Thee and am not worthy to be called Thy son." Two large tears rolled down the old man's cheeks.

Early the next morning, he stood watching the

"FATHER, I HAVE SINNED AGAINST HEAVEN AND BEFORE THEE"

fresh, bright sun gild mountain and valley. The sound of a few early bells reached him and birds sang their morning song in the fir trees. He called, "Come along, Heidi. Put on your best frock. We are going to church."

Soon, she came down wearing her Frankfurt dress. "Why, Grandfather, I never saw you look like that before! Your Sunday coat has silver buttons!"

He just smiled, and together they walked down the mountain, entered Dorfli church, and sat in the back. Whispers started. "Do you see? Alm-Uncle is in church!" Everybody grew more attentive when the sermon began. The preacher spoke thankfully, as if some great joy had come to them all.

At the close of service, Grandfather and Heidi followed the pastor to his house. Alm-Uncle shook hands with the pastor and begged forgiveness. "You were right. I was wrong. We will live in Dorfli this winter. The child is not strong enough to stand the

"YOU WERE RIGHT. I WAS WRONG"

bitter mountain cold. If people here feel I am not to be trusted, it is my own fault. You, I am sure, will not do so."

The pastor's eyes shone with pleasure. "Neighbor, I am greatly rejoiced. I look forward to spending many pleasant winter evenings together. We shall find friends for the little one, too." He patted her curly head.

Outside, the congregation that had bitterly condemned the prodigal came to welcome him. A great chorus of pleasure arose when people learned that Alm-Uncle would be in Dorfli for the winter. He told Heidi on the way home, "I am happier today than I deserve; happier than I thought possible. It is good to be at peace with God and man. God was good to me when He sent you to my hut."

At Peter's home, the grandfather walked straight in. "Good morning, Grandmother. We shall have to do some patching up before the autumn winds come."

"IT IS GOOD TO BE AT PEACE WITH GOD AND MAN"

"Dear God, if it is not Uncle!" she cried in pleased surprise. "Now, I can thank you for all you have done for me. I have something on my heart. If I have injured you in any way, do not punish me by sending the child away. You do not know what she is to me!" She clasped Heidi to her.

"Have no fear, Grandmother," he reassured. "I shall not punish either you or myself by doing so. We are all together now. Pray God we may continue."

Just then, Peter rushed in with a letter from Clara. She said the house had been dull since Heidi had left. In the coming autumn, her father and Grandmamma would bring her to the baths at Ragatz and for a visit on the mountain.

Some time later in Frankfurt, the kindly doctor walked along the street to the Sesemanns' looking sad. His only daughter had died a few months before.

PETER RUSHED IN WITH A LETTER FROM CLARA

He found his friend distraught. The past summer had been Clara's worst in years. Yet, she clung to the promise of the Swiss journey.

"Impossible!" the doctor said with authority. "Not until next summer."

"Do you really have any hope of her final recovery?"

"Very little. Yet, you still have a beloved child. Think of my lonely house."

Herr Sesemann strode up and down. "Doctor, I cannot bear to see you look so. You shall take the journey and visit Heidi."

The doctor objected, but later, when Clara turned blue, tear-filled eyes toward him and pleaded with him to go, he gave in. She packed boxes of gifts, including soft cakes, a warm, hooded cloak for Heidi, a thick shawl for the grandmother, and an immense sausage, sent to Brigitta so Peter wouldn't

" YOU SHALL TAKE THE JOURNEY AND VISIT HEIDI "

eat it all at once!

One afternoon, the doctor climbed the mountain, so lonely he didn't see its beauty. Heidi and the grandfather's warm reception lifted his spirits.

Heidi felt disappointed that Clara could not come until spring but was glad to see her doctor friend. Soon, a man arrived with the presents, and she cried with wonder and delight. They took the gifts to Peter's, and Heidi stayed while Peter's family stood speechless at the sight of the good things to eat. Grandmother stroked the shawl whose thickness would keep her warm in winter.

The next day, the doctor climbed with Peter, Heidi, and the goats. He asked her how a sad heart could see the beauty. She told him to tell everything to God, and that saying Grandmother's hymns had brought the light back. She repeated a hymn beginning, "Let not your heart be troubled." It ended by saying to wait and not doubt. The doctor brightened.

HE ASKED HER HOW A SAD HEART COULD SEE THE BEAUTY

HEIDI

Peter did not. Heidi hadn't gone with him for days. Now, she spent all the time talking to the doctor. Peter flew into a terrible temper. He stood behind the doctor, made faces, and doubled his fists. When they opened the dinner bag, and Heidi gave Peter most of it, he felt guilty. Before he would eat, he sprang back behind the doctor and held up his open hands as a sign he no longer wished to use them as fists.

On the last of September, the doctor left for Frankfurt. He wanted to take Heidi with him. She thought of its rows of endless houses, its hard streets, and even of Fraulein Rottenmeier. Then, she saw the old sadness in the doctor's eyes and sobbed, " I will come, but first I must tell Grandfather."

"No child, not now," the doctor said kindly. "But if I am ever ill and alone, will you come and stay with me?"

"Yes, for I love you nearly as much as Grandfather."

"I LOVE YOU NEARLY AS MUCH AS GRANDFATHER"

As he turned for a last glimpse of the waving Heidi, and the sunny mountain, he said to himself, "It is good for body and soul to be up there. A man might learn how to be happy once more."

"A MAN MIGHT LEARN HOW TO BE HAPPY ONCE MORE"

PETER SANK ALMOST TO HIS SHOULDERS

8
Winter in Dorfli

Snow lay so high around the hut, the windows looked level with the ground. The door had entirely disappeared. Fresh snow fell every night. Each morning, Peter crawled out of the sitting-room window and immediately sank almost to his shoulders. He struggled with hands, feet, and head to free himself. With a large broom, he worked hard to make a path to the door.

Sometimes, the fresh snow froze in the night, and Peter stepped through the window onto hard, smooth snowbanks. He could slide to Dorfli any way he chose. The whole mountain was a wide, unbroken sleigh road.

Alm-Uncle had kept his word. He rented a half-ruined building near the church, overgrown with ivy and large enough to partition. He covered the floor of one side with straw and made a goats' house. All autumn he worked, restoring what had once been a fine home. The immense stove in the corner nearly reached the ceiling. Blue pictures of old castles and quiet lakes were painted on its white tiles. A seat ran all around it. A large space between the stove and wall became Heidi's room. The old man put four large planks there to hold her hay bed.

She delighted in all the rooms, but on the fourth morning, she jumped up and said, "I must go see the grandmother."

Grandfather shook his head. "Neither today nor tomorrow. The mountain is fathom-deep in snow, and it is still falling. Even sturdy Peter can hardly get along. Wait till it freezes, then you will be able to walk over the hard snow."

She didn't like to wait, but her days were busy. Heidi went to school and eagerly set to work. She hardly ever saw Peter, who was usually absent from

"THE MOUNTAIN IS FATHOM-DEEP IN SNOW"

school. The teacher merely remarked, "I daresay he cannot come in the snow." Yet, Peter managed to get through most evenings for a visit with Heidi!

Finally, the sun shone brightly over the white ground, although it went to bed behind the mountains early. The great moon came out. The next morning, the whole mountain glistened like a huge crystal. When Peter got out the window, he fell on the hard snow and slid down the mountainside like a sleigh on the iron-hard ground! "I must be off to school," he said.

"Go and learn all you can," the grandmother encouraged.

Peter's sleigh shot down like lightning. Past Dorfli. Past Mayenfeld. Too late to go to school. It would take him a good hour to walk back to Dorfli. He took his time going and marched in as Heidi and her grandfather sat at dinner.

"Why weren't you at school today? You could

PETER'S SLEIGH SHOT DOWN LIKE LIGTHNING

have come on the sleigh," she said reproachfully. "The frost is here, and I can go see Grandmother."

"My sleigh carried me on too far, and I was too late."

"I call that being a deserter," said the Uncle. "An army leader like yourself ought to be ashamed of running away. What would you think of your goats if one went this way, another that way, and they refused to follow? What would you do?"

"I should beat them," Peter said.

"If a boy behaved like the unruly goats and were punished, what then?"

"Serves him right," came the answer.

"Good. Next time you let your sleigh carry you past the school when you ought to be inside at your lessons, come on to me afterwards and receive what you deserve."

Peter looked fearful, in awe of the Alm-Uncle.

"Come have something to eat, and afterwards

"COME TO ME AFTERWARDS AND RECEIVE WHAT YOU DESERVE"

Heidi shall go with you. Bring her back this evening, and you will find supper waiting for you."

This unexpected turn of conversation set Peter to grinning. Heidi excitedly pushed potatoes and toasted cheese toward him then ran for the warm hooded cloak Clara had sent. They chattered all the way up the mountain. Peter admitted he'd rather go to school than get what Uncle threatened!

"Thank God," the grandmother cried when Heidi ran into the cottage. She had held a secret fear all autumn that the strange gentleman who had visited would spirit Heidi away. Now, she shivered with cold in spite of the warm, gray shawl. "The frost has got into my bones a bit, but perhaps tomorrow I shall feel better and get back to my spinning."

"Grandmother, your bed is wrong. It goes downhill at your head and not up."

"I know. I have lain on my pillow so many years, it has grown flat. But we will not talk of that. I have

HE'D RATHER GO TO SCHOOL THAN GET WHAT UNCLE THREATENED!

so much other sick people are without. I thank God for the bread I get every day, and this warm wrap, and your visits. Will you read me something?"

Heidi fetched the hymn book. The Grandmother lay with folded hands, peace stealing over her worn, troubled face like one hearing good news.

"Grandmother, are you feeling better?"

"Yes, child. Go on." After Heidi closed the book, the grandmother repeated, *"As the eyes grow dim, and darkness closes round, the soul grows clearer; sees the goal to which it travels, gladly feels its home is nearer."* She added, "Even when I lie here alone in silence and darkness, feeling it will never be light again, I am comforted by the words you read."

Heidi and Peter darted down the mountainside on the sleigh under the bright moon. That night on her bed of hay, Heidi thought, if I could read to the grandmother every day, I could make her feel better. But I cannot go up the mountain again for a week,

"I AM COMFORTED BY THE WORDS YOU READ"

if not two. Suddenly, an idea so delightful she could hardly wait till morning struck her. She sat upright in bed and prayed with all her heart.

Peter arrived punctually at school the following day. Afterwards he walked into the large room at Uncle's. Heidi rushed forward and took hold of him. "Peter, you must learn to read."

"I have."

"Yes, but so you can really make use of it. Nobody believes you can't learn. I will teach you to read. You must learn at once, then you can read hymns every day to Grandmother."

"I don't care about that," he grumbled.

His hard-hearted way of refusing to agree to what was right and kind aroused Heidi's anger. "If you won't learn, I will tell you what will happen. Your mother has spoken often of sending you to Frankfurt. Clara pointed out where boys and even grown men go for lessons. There are ever so many teachers,

"PETER, YOU MUST LEARN TO READ"

dressed in black with high black hats."

Peter felt a cold shudder run down his back.

"When it comes your turn you won't be able to read. They will make fun of you, even worse than Tinette, and you should have seen her."

"I'll learn then," he sullenly said.

"We will begin at once." Heidi dragged him to the table and brought out an ABC book with rhyming lines that served capitally for teaching Peter. She made him spell out the first sentence two or three times. When he didn't get it at first, she read the rhyme that threatened all kinds of punishment to those who didn't learn their ABC's. She paused after reading "'Now R S T be quick about or worse will follow, there's little doubt.'" Peter sat petrified and stared at her with horror-stricken eyes. She quickly reassured, "You need not be afraid. Come here to me every evening. If you learn as you have today, you will at last know all your letters. You

"I'LL LEARN THEN"

must come regularly; even if it snows, it won't hurt you."

Peter promised. His fears had made him tame and docile. Every evening, he diligently worked. The grandfather frequently hid sudden fits of merriment, but often invited Peter to stay to supper after his great exertion.

One evening Heidi read, "'If you falter at W, worst of all, look at the stick against the wall.'"

Peter looked at the wall and said scornfully, "There isn't one."

"Yes, but do you know what Grandfather has in his box? A stick almost as thick as your arm." Peter knew that thick hazel stick and immediately struggled to master the W.

Day after day, he studied until the frost had gone and the snow lay soft. Fresh snow made it impossible for Heidi to visit the grandmother. She pursued her teaching even more eagerly until one evening, Peter

DAY AFTER DAY, HE STUDIED

told his mother and grandmother, "I can read now." He brought the hymn book and read a hymn through, to the surprise and delight of his family.

The next day during a reading lesson in Peter's class, it came his turn. The teacher said, "We must pass over Peter as usual—or will you try once more to stammer through a sentence?"

Peter took the book and read off three lines without the slightest hesitation.

The teacher stared. "Peter, I have been striving to teach you with unheard-of patience but made up my mind not to waste any more time. How has such a miracle come to pass in our days?"

"It was Heidi."

The teacher looked astonished. "And who has wrought the change in you, that you have not lately stayed away a single day?"

"It was Uncle," Peter answered and read off another three lines. When school closed, the teacher

"HOW HAS SUCH A MIRACLE COME TO PASS IN OUR DAYS?"

ran to the pastor to tell him the good news. Every evening, Peter read one hymn to the grandmother. Yet, they never sounded the same as when Heidi read them. Peter arranged to make his reading as little troublesome as possible and left out the long difficult words!

EVERY EVENING, PETER READ ONE HYMN TO THE GRANDMOTHER

"FROM CLARA!"

9
A New Life for Clara

May brought full fresh streams of spring flowing into the valley. Clear, warm sunshine turned the mountain green again and coaxed bright flowers where deep snows had lain. Winds sang through the fir trees and lulled Heidi to sleep. She danced in the wind and rejoiced at being home. Grandfather busily made new chairs for the summer visitors.

Peter's whistle broke into an evening conversation. Heidi ran out and found herself surrounded by her four-footed friends. Peter sent them flying right and left. "There!" he exclaimed and handed her a letter.

"From Clara!" She quickly read,

"*Dearest Heidi,*
    Everything is packed. Every day, the doctor comes and cries, 'Off now as quickly as

*you can to the mountain.' You cannot think
how much he enjoyed himself with you. He
says no one can help getting well up there.
He looks quite young and happy again since
his visit. Oh, how I am looking forward to
coming and meeting Peter and the goats.*

*"First I must go through a six weeks' cure
at Ragatz, then we shall move to Dorfli.
Every fine day, I shall be carried up the
mountain and spend the day with you.
Grandmamma is coming and will remain
with me. Fraulein Rottenmeier refuses to
come. So does Tinette. Sebastian gave a
frightful description of rocks so dangerous
and overhanging, you might fall in a cre-
vasse. I can hardly bear waiting till I see you
again."*

When Heidi finished, Peter rushed out twirling
his stick. He chased his goats down the mountain in

" ' EVERY FINE DAY, I SHALL SPEND WITH YOU ' "

great leaps, as if longing to vent his fury on an invisible foe—the Frankfurt visitors.

Heidi visited the grandmother the following day to tell the good news. The old woman was no longer confined to bed but back in her corner spinning. She wore a mournful look. Peter had told her the night before about the Sesemanns' coming. Grandmother had not slept at all for fear they would take Heidi away from the mountain. Now, Heidi read a comforting hymn. *"All things will work for good to those who trust in Me; I come with healing on my wings, to save and set thee free."*

"Yes, that is just what I wanted to hear." The trouble left Grandmother's face.

May passed, a month of glorious stars and bright, cloudless days. June came with even hotter sun. One day near its close, Heidi finished her duties and ran outside. The rock roses should be open now. She would go see. Just as she turned the corner of the

"YES, THAT IS JUST WHAT I WANTED TO HEAR"

hut, she gave such a loud cry, Grandfather hurried out of the shed to see what had happened.

A strange procession made its way up the mountain. In front, two men carried a sedan chair holding a girl well wrapped in shawls. A horse followed, mounted by a stately looking lady talking to the guide who walked beside her. Next, came a man pushing a reclining chair and finally, a porter. He bore such a bundle of cloaks, shawls, and furs on his back it rose well above his head.

"They've come!" Heidi rushed forward to greet Clara then Grandmamma.

"What a magnificent residence you have, Uncle," the old lady burst out. "A king might well envy you. And my little Heidi, she is well and looks like a wild rose."

Clara stared. Never had she seen such beauty. "I should like to remain here forever."

The grandfather spread wraps over the invalid

" I SHOULD LIKE TO REMAIN HERE FOREVER "

chair, lifted Clara and laid her gently down on her own couch.

"You are a wonderful nurse," Grandmamma told him.

A spasm of pain crossed his face. He remembered his captain while fighting in Sicily. Crippled and unable to move, he had suffered no one but Uncle to nurse him until his sufferings had ended in death.

"Oh, Heidi, if only I could walk about with you." Clara said longingly. Heidi immediately pushed Clara's chair around the hut to the lofty fir trees whose splendid tops pointed toward heaven. Next, they visited the goat shed. Clara lamented its emptiness but cried out at the flowers.

Heidi picked a great bouquet and said, "If you could come up where the goats feed, you would see so many more, especially the yellow rock roses that gleam like pure gold and smell so lovely! I am sure I could push you up, the chair goes so easily." She

THEY VISITED THE GOAT SHED

sent the chair at such a pace around the corner, it nearly went flying down the mountainside, but Grandmamma stopped it.

Grandfather put the table and extra seats by the outdoor seat and brought the cheese and milk. Grandmamma said she had never enjoyed anything so much. "Clara, are you having a second piece of cheese?" she cried, amazed.

"Yes. Everything tastes so much better here." She bit into the golden slice.

But when the sun began its descent, and Grandmamma said they must go, her face fell. "Oh, we haven't seen inside the hut or Heidi's bed. If only the day were ten hours long!" They rose, and Uncle carried Clara inside and up the ladder to the hayloft.

Clara was charmed. "Your room is wonderful. Why, you can look from your bed straight into the sky and outside the fir trees wave and rustle."

Uncle looked at Grandmamma. "If you agree,

"EVERYTHING TASTES SO MUCH BETTER HERE"

your little granddaughter might remain up here and grow stronger. We can make a soft bed of the shawls and covers you brought, and I'll see to it the general looks after her."

The grandmother heartily agreed, and the girls clapped their hands in delight when Grandfather said Clara should stay at least a month! Grandmamma would go to Ragatz but make excursions up the mountain now and then, so Grandfather accompanied her down the precipitous mountain path.

Before he returned, Peter arrived with the goats. Clara made her long-wished-for acquaintance with little Snowflake, the lively Greenfinch, Little Swan, and Little Bear, and even the Grand Turk. Peter stood back casting unfriendly glances at her and didn't answer when the girls called, "Good evening." He ran off angrily swinging his stick with his goats after him.

That night, Clara lay on the large soft bed in the

YOUR GRANDDAUGHTER MIGHT REMAIN HERE AND GROW STRONGER

hayloft next to Heidi. She looked out the round open window into the shining clusters of stars and exclaimed, "It's as if we were in a high carriage and were going to drive straight into heaven."

"Do you know why the stars are so happy and look down and nod to us? It's because they live up in heaven. They know how well God arranges everything for us so we need have no more fear and trouble and may be quite sure all things will come right in the end. We must never forget to pray, so we may feel safe and have no anxiety about what is going to happen."

After they said their prayers and Heidi fell asleep, Clara lay awake. She had seldom seen a star and felt she could not look at them long enough.

She awakened to a new and delightful, sunny world. She had never tasted goat's milk before, but Grandfather said it would make her strong. He ordered Peter to let Little Swan climb where she

"THEY KNOW HOW WELL GOD ARRANGES EVERYTHING..."

liked to find the best food, so she would give the finest milk possible.

Peter marched away, angry when Heidi said, "I cannot come for a long, long time—not as long as Clara is with me. However, Grandfather has promised to go up the mountain with both of us one day." Peter doubled his fists and made threatening gestures toward the invalid on her couch then hurried out of sight for fear Uncle had seen him. He came down that evening still scowling and took no notice when Heidi and Clara called to him but went on with his goats.

On the third day, two stout porters arrived, each carrying a bed with bedding of all kinds and beautiful white coverlids. A letter from Grandmamma said when Heidi would go to Dorfli in the winter, she was to take one bed with her. She must always leave the other at the hut, so Clara would know her bed waited when she visited the mountain. Grandfather threw

PETER MADE THREATENING GESTURES

back the hay and put the beds close together by the window, so they could see the sun and stars.

By the end of the third week, Grandfather had persuaded Clara to stand for a minute or two. She tried in order to please him, but clung to him. "It hurts so when my feet touch the ground." Still, he had her try a little longer each day. Her dream was to go up to the beautiful flowers where she could see the wonderful light from the evening sun.

Heidi also longed to see it again. "Grandfather, will you take us out with the goats tomorrow? Oh, it is so lovely up there now!"

"Very well," he answered. "But if I do, the little daughter must do something to please me. She must try her best again this evening to stand on her feet." Clara promised. Heidi was so pleased and excited she called to Peter the minute she caught sight of him that evening, "Peter, we are all coming out with you tomorrow and are going to stay up there the whole day."

"SHE MUST TRY HER BEST TO STAND ON HER OWN FEET"

Peter, cross as a bear, grumbled a reply, and lifted his stick, but the goats danced out of the way, and the stick only hit the air.

That night, Clara dreamed of an immense sky-colored field with bell-shaped flowers, and Heidi heard the great bird of prey call from the heights, "Come!"

HEIDI HEARD THE GREAT BIRD OF PREY CALL FROM THE HEIGHTS

PIECES FLEW IN EVERY DIRECTION

10
A Bad Time for Peter

Peter's anger and bitterness reached high pitch. For weeks, he had not had Heidi to himself. Every time he came, the invalid always sat in her chair. One morning, the hated chair stood by the hut door. Peter glanced around to be sure no one could see him. Then he sprang forward like a wild creature and gave it a violent push!

Peter sped up the mountain and crouched in the shelter of a large blackberry bush. The chair rolled faster and faster. It turned over several times. Pieces flew in every direction. Peter leaped in the air, laughing and stamping with joy. Now Heidi's friend would go away, and she would come out with him.

Below him, Grandfather and Heidi searched for the chair, with no success. Grandfather took Clara up the mountain. Heidi followed with the goats.

HEIDI

Grandfather scolded Peter. "I'll teach you to go by like that, you lazy rascal! What do you mean by it? Have you seen the chair?"

"What chair?"

Uncle said no more. He made Clara comfortable then left, promising to come fetch Clara and Heidi that evening.

Not a single cloud sailed in the dark, blue sky. The great snow field sparkled. Now and then a goat came to lie down beside the children. Some hours went by, and Heidi said, "Would you think me unkind if I went to see how the flowers are looking?"

She brought green leaves and left Snowflake to keep Clara company. While Heidi was gone, Clara found pleasure in being alone with a little goat that looked to her for protection. She suddenly felt a great desire to help others instead of always being dependent as she was now.

Heidi reached the gorgeous field of flowers. She

"HAVE YOU SEEN THE CHAIR?"

breathlessly ran back to Clara. "Oh, you must come! I believe I could carry you."

"If only I could walk. You are too small to carry me." Clara looked sad.

"Peter, you must come help me," Heidi ordered.

"I shall do nothing of the kind," was the surly answer.

"Then I shall do something you won't like."

Fear raced through Peter. Did she suspect? What would Alm-Uncle do if he discovered what Peter had done to the chair? "I am coming." Between them, they got Clara to her feet. She tried to stand, but drew quickly back.

"Put your foot down firmly once," said Heidi. "It will hurt less after that."

Clara followed Heidi's advice and ventured a step, then another. Each step hurt less. She shouted, "Look! Heidi, *I can walk!*" She still hung onto her supports and soon they reached the flowers, the girls

"LOOK! HEIDI, I CAN WALK!"

rejoicing. Peter fell asleep and dreamed he saw the beautiful red-padded chair standing uninjured by the grandfather's door. Again, dreadful fear fell over him.

Heidi's threat had not concerned the chair. She had only meant to withhold dinner if he didn't help, but Peter's conscience tormented him.

In Dorfli that evening, a large group of people stood by the last thing Peter wanted to see: the remains of Clara's wheelchair.

"It was worth a good twenty-five pounds," the baker said. "The gentleman from Frankfurt will make inquiries. I am glad I haven't been seen up the mountain for two years. Suspicion will fall on anyone up there at the time."

Frightened and trembling, Peter crept away and ran home. He behaved like the Great Turk when he thought somebody was after him with a stick. Every day, Peter expected the constable from Frankfurt to

FRIGHTENED AND TREMBLING, PETER CREPT AWAY

leap out on him from behind some bush or hedge.

Heidi and Clara agreed they were happy God answered prayers the best way and not just the way they asked Him. Every day Clara walked more, and they wrote, and invited Grandmamma to come see them.

Grandmamma cried with joy over Clara. "Uncle, this is all your doing."

"And God's good sun and mountain air." He smiled.

"Don't forget the goat's milk," Clara put in.

"I must telegraph my son in Paris immediately."

"I will fetch Peter." Uncle went aside a little way and blew such a resounding whistle Peter pelted down, white as a ghost, relieved it was just an errand.

Meanwhile, Herr Sesemann had traveled to Dorfli and started up the mountain as a surprise. He met Peter and asked directions. Peter turned away in

"UNCLE, THIS IS ALL YOUR DOING"

such haste, he fell head over heels and went rolling just as the chair had done. Herr Sesemann stared and climbed on, but Peter suffered from far more than his tumble. The stranger who had asked the way to the mountain must be the Frankfurt policeman! Limping, groaning, afraid to disobey Uncle, he lagged back up the trail toward the hut.

Herr Sesemann's heart leaped when Heidi and a tall, fair girl who looked exactly like her mother walked toward him!

"How is it possible?" He clasped her in his arms. "Clara, my dear Clara!"

A slight rustling announced Peter's presence when he tried to slip by unobserved. "Come along, boy," Grandmamma called.

Peter stepped from behind the fir tree, face pale and distorted with terror. He saw Uncle with his terrible gray eyes and the police-constable from Frankfurt.

"CLARA, MY DEAR CLARA!"

"It can never be put back together again," he confessed in a whisper. "Peter was the wind that sent the chair rolling. He is expecting his well-deserved punishment," Uncle said.

The old lady said firmly, "We will punish him no more. We have claimed Heidi's company and taken away his only possession. He acted foolishly while angry, as we all have. Come here, boy. Listen to me. You did a wrong thing and have been trying to hide it. Peter, you cannot hide from God. He wakes up the little watchman He places inside us when we are born, and who sleeps quietly till we do something wrong. When he wakes he calls, 'Now you will be found out, dragged off, and punished.' Is that how you felt?"

Peter nodded contritely.

"Clara had no chair but wanted to see the flowers and made the effort. Now she can walk. God is able to bring good out of evil. Will you remember that?

"PETER, YOU CANNOT HIDE FROM GOD"

When you are tempted to do wrong, will you remember the little watchman and his disagreeable voice?" Peter solemnly promised.

"Then it's over and done with. I want you to have a pleasant reminder of the Frankfurt visitors. What would you like?"

Peter's mind whirled. Instead of punishment, he would have a present! He thought of the fair in Mayenfeld, of red whistles, splendid knives. "A penny."

Grandmamma put four bright round shillings in his hand then laid some pennies on top. "Every Sunday throughout the year, you can take out a penny to spend."

"As long as I live?" Peter innocently asked.

Grandmamma laughed. "I will put it in my will."

"Thank God!" Peter ran off in great joy.

Herr Sesemann turned to the grandfather. "How can we show our gratitude?"

"AS LONG AS I LIVE?"

HEIDI

With dignity, the Alm-Uncle replied, "I have received my payment in joy of Clara's recovery. I have but one wish. I am growing old and have nothing to leave the child when I die."

"I look upon her as our own, and she shall be treated so during my life and after. She is unfitted to live away from home, but my friend the doctor is going to settle in this neighborhood. The child will have two protectors near her—and may they both live long to share the task!"

"God grant that indeed it may be so," Grandmamma turned to Heidi. "Is there anything you particularly wish for?"

"Yes." She clapped. "May Grandmother have my bed from Frankfurt?"

Grandmamma nodded, and Heidi started off but Grandfather reproved her. "We have company."

"We will go tell Grandmother together," Frau Sesemann said.

"THE CHILD WILL HAVE TWO PROTECTORS NEAR HER"

HEIDI

Heidi rushed inside the cottage when they arrived, telling about the wonderful bed. Grandmother sadly smiled. "She must indeed be a kind lady but alas, I shall not live long once she takes you."

Frau Sesemann said, "Such tales! Heidi is staying here with you. Each year we shall visit the Alm to offer special thanks to God for the miracle of Clara's healing."

Tears of joy rolled. Heidi clung to the grandmother. "It's just like the hymn."

"Yes. Nothing strengthens our belief in a kind heavenly Father who never forgets even the least of His creatures so much as people filled with love for poor useless creatures such as I."

"We are all equally poor and helpless in the eyes of God," Frau Sesemann told her. "Good-bye until next year."

The next day, Clara left with her father and grandmother amidst tears and promises to come back the next summer.

"WE ARE ALL EQUALLY POOR AND HELPLESS IN THE EYES OF GOD"

HEIDI

Now the bed has arrived. Grandmother sleeps soundly and is sure to grow stronger, warmed by clothing sent by the Frau Sesemann.

The doctor is restoring the magnificent old Dorfli house, part for him and part for Heidi and Grandfather in winter. A warm, walled stall is for the goats.

One evening, the doctor said to his new friend, "Heidi has the same claims on me as if she were my own child. We shall be able to leave her without anxiety when the day comes that you and I must go."

Uncle silently clasped the doctor's hand, his eyes showing gladness.

Heidi and Peter at that moment sat with Grandmother and Brigitta, faces glowing. At last the grandmother spoke, "Heidi, read me one of the hymns. I feel I can do nothing for the remainder of my life but thank our Father in Heaven for all the mercies He has shown us!"

"I FEEL I CAN DO NOTHING BUT THANK OUR FATHER IN HEAVEN"

POLLYANNA

SAMUEL MORRIS

Thrilling
Real-life
Drama

AT A BOOKSTORE NEAR YOU!